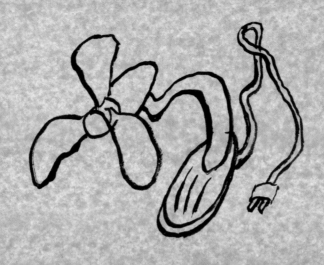 

W9-COL-974

  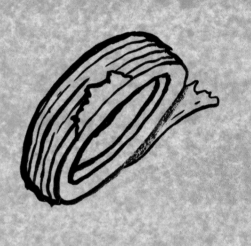

 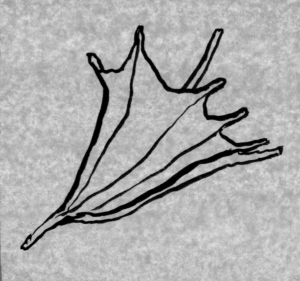 

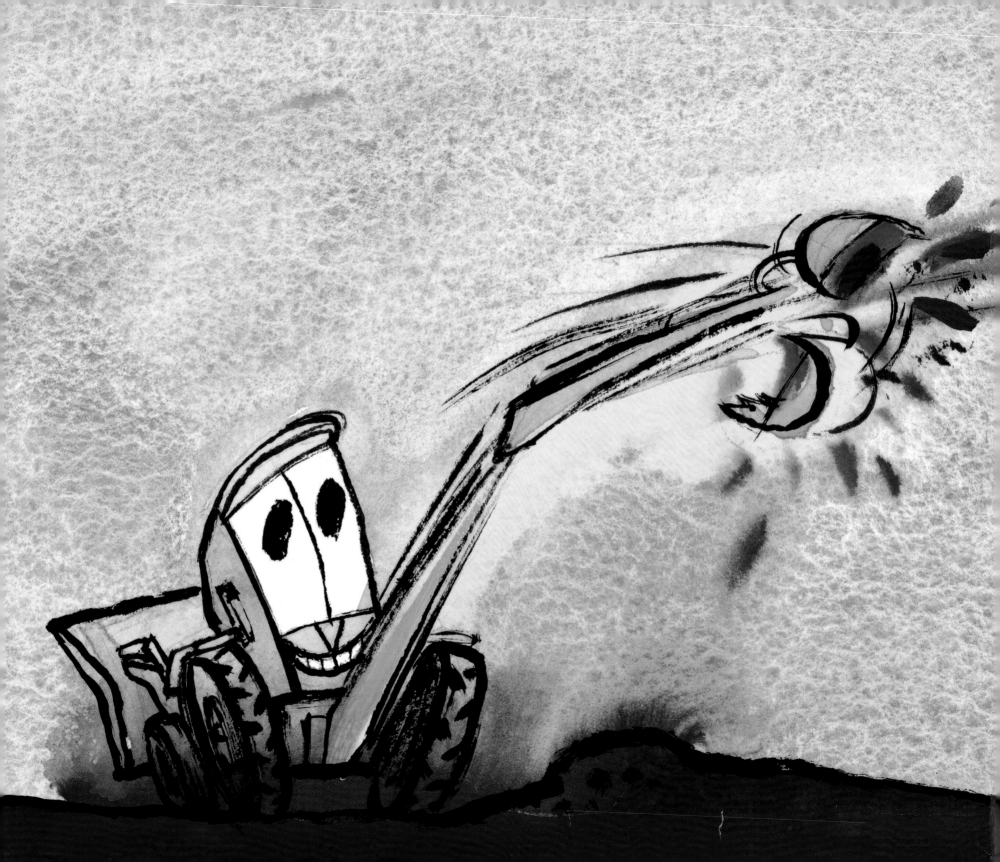

I'M DIRTY!

KATE & JIM McMULLAN

SOMERSET CO. LIBRARY
BRIDGEWATER, N.J. 08807

JOANNA COTLER BOOKS

An Imprint of HarperCollinsPublishers

I'm Dirty! Text copyright © 2006 by Kate McMullan Illustrations copyright © 2006 by Jim McMullan Manufactured in China. All rights reserved. www.harpercollinschildrens.com Library of Congress Cataloging-in-Publication Data McMullan, Kate. I'm dirty! / Kate & Jim McMullan.— 1st ed. p. cm. Summary: A busy backhoe loader describes all the items it hauls off of a lot and all the fun it has getting dirty while doing so. ISBN-10: 0-06-009293-9 (trade bdg.) — ISBN-13: 978-0-06-009293-1 (trade bdg.) ISBN-10: 0-06-009294-7 (lib. bdg.) — ISBN-13: 978-0-06-009294-8 (lib. bdg.) [1. Backhoes—Fiction. 2. Cleanliness—Fiction.] I. Title: I am dirty!. II. McMullan, Jim, date III. Title. PZ7.M47879Ik 2006 2005017919 [E]—dc22 Typography by Neil Swaab 1 2 3 4 5 6 7 8 9 10 ❖ First Edition

For backhoe ace Michael Steiner

A great big load of thanks to the HarperCollins Crew:
Joanna Cotler, Justin Chanda, Alyson Day,
Neil Swaab, Ruiko Tokunaga, Karen Nagel, and Kathryn Silsand.
Also to Mindy Reyer, Jacqueline Moss, Peter Field,
and the kids at the Morris Center School;
Dan Steiger and Meridith Nadler;
Bill Villano at One Source Tools;
Antonio, Daphne, Gemma, and Paolo Caglioti;
and to my first-prize, cross-your-eyes Pippins,
Holly McGhee and Emily van Beek.

Who's got
a BOOM,
a dipper stick,
and a BUCKET
with a row of chompers?

ME!

Up *FRONT,*

Counting down

10 torn-up truck tires

9 fractured fans

what I'm cleaning up:

8 busted beach
umbrellas

7 loused-up
lawn chairs

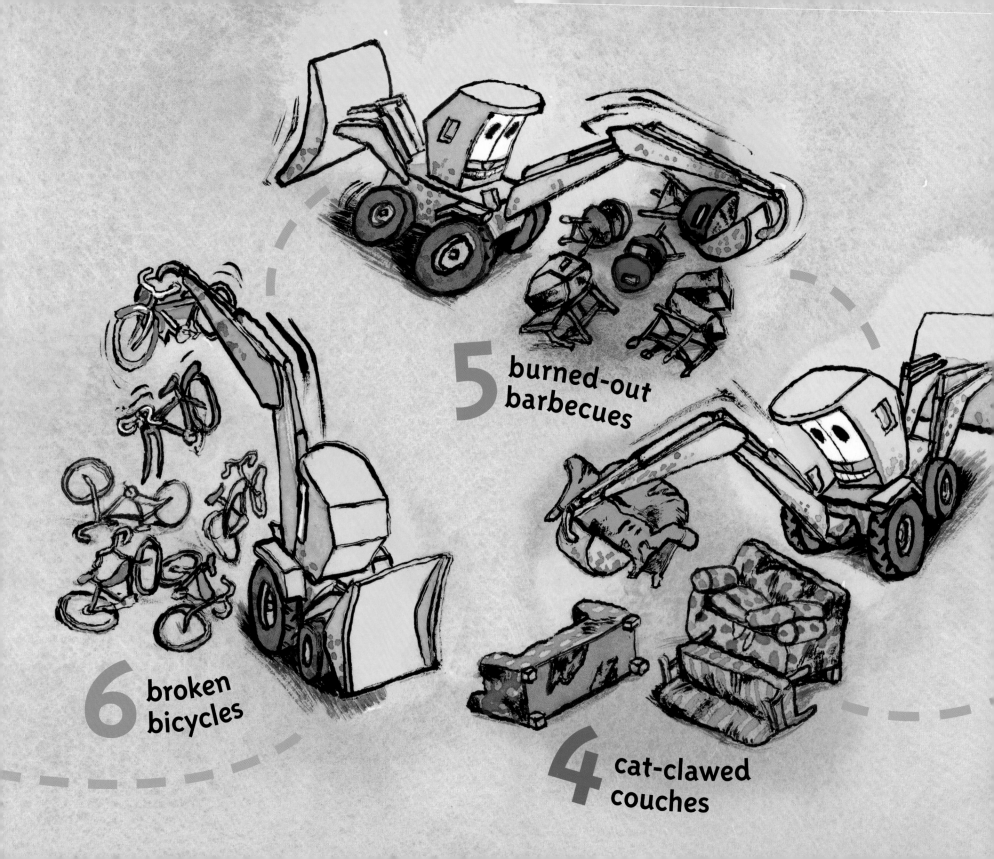

5 burned-out barbecues

6 broken bicycles

4 cat-clawed couches

Dumpster time . . .

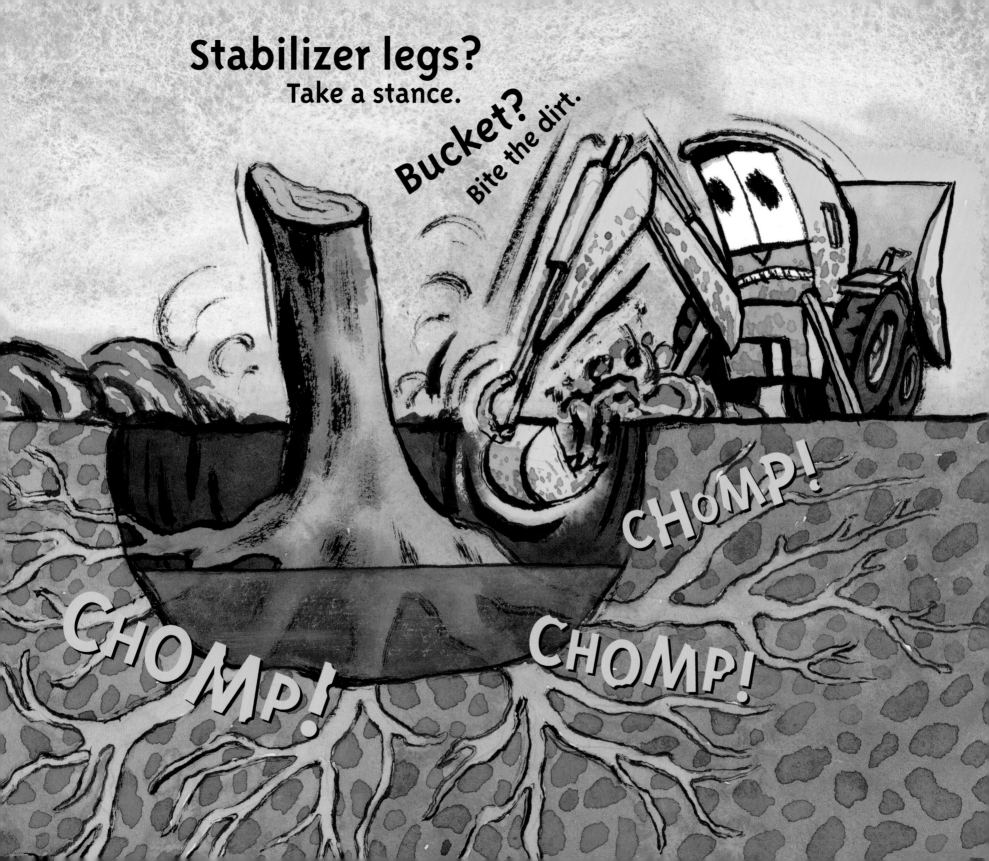

This lot's cleaned up.
And me?
I'm DIRTY.

Backhoe Loader, signing off.

Have a
dirty day!

Picture MCMULLAN
McMullan, Kate.
I'm dirty!

2/6/07

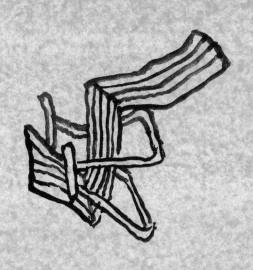

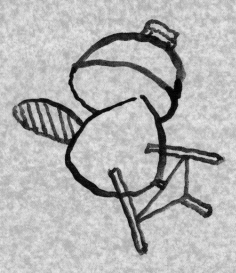